DOGGY DARE

Books in the Animal Ark Pets series

BEN M. BAGLIO

DOGGY DARE

Illustrated by
Paul Howard

Cover Illustration by
Chris Chapman

A
LITTLE APPLE
PAPERBACK

SCHOLASTIC INC.
New York Toronto London Auckland Sydney
Mexico City New Delhi Hong Kong

Special thanks to Mary Hooper.

ISBN 0-439-05169-X

12 11 10 9 8 7 6 5
1 2 3 4 5/0

Printed in the U.S.A.
40

First Scholastic Trade printing, August 2000

Contents

DOGGY DARE

1

The Newcomers

Mandy Hope stood outside Welford's general store with James Hunter. "Who's that?" she asked, nodding toward a boy standing on the other side of the road.

James untied Blackie's leash from the railing. He looked over at the boy and shook his head.

"I don't know," he said. "I've never seen him before."

The two of them stared as the boy glanced at a comic book, then stuffed it into a bag he was carrying. Mandy was about to say hello, but the boy didn't look over at them. Instead he walked off, crossing the road farther up Main Street.

"It's no one from school," Mandy said. "No one I recognize at all."

"He's probably just a visitor," said James. "Honestly, Mandy, you are so nosy!"

Mandy smiled. "I just like to know what's going on!"

The two friends stood on the sidewalk ready to cross the street. James patted his side to get Blackie to sit down next to him.

"We're crossing the road, Blackie," he said. "Look carefully before you cross."

But Blackie didn't sit. Instead the black Labrador jumped up and shoved his nose into the bag of lemon drops that James had just bought.

"No, you don't!" James said, "not yet. You only get a reward if you walk across the street correctly. You must heel."

"You'd better not let him have too many sweets," Mandy said. "They're bad for his teeth."

Mandy's mom and dad were both vets. Mandy hoped to be a vet one day, too. In the meantime, she loved animals and had as much to do with them as she possibly could. James always said that there wasn't a pet in Welford that Mandy didn't know by name.

"They're bad for *your* teeth," James said, "but that doesn't stop you eating them, does it?"

"That's different," Mandy said.

On the other side of the street James gave Blackie a doggy treat for being good. He gulped it down, then looked at James for another.

"Not yet," James said. Besides trying to save Blackie's teeth, James was trying to train his dog to be obedient. If Blackie did what he was told, then he got a treat as a reward.

Mandy looked up the street. "There's that boy again," she said. "He just went into the grocery store and now he's come out."

"Let's catch up to him and talk to him," James said. "He might be new here."

"Yes, perhaps he — oh, he's got a dog!" Mandy said with delight. A small, scruffy mixed breed suddenly appeared out of the shop doorway and began to walk behind the boy.

The boy stopped and spoke to the dog, then bent to pet him.

"I don't think I've seen that dog before, either," Mandy said.

"There's a mystery for you," James said, popping a lemon drop in his mouth and offering the bag to Mandy. "A strange boy and a strange dog."

Blackie jumped for the paper bag again and knocked it onto the sidewalk. James had to sit him down and scold him. By the time Mandy and James started walking again, the mystery boy was almost at the end of Main Street. He was about to turn onto a road that led to one of the farms.

"He *must* be a stranger," James said. "If he wasn't, he'd know not to go down there. With all the rain we've had lately the road is a swamp. Farther down the mud's a foot deep."

Mandy nodded. "My dad said that only tractors could get through to the farm now." She screwed up her eyes in order to see the small figure more clearly. "And it doesn't look as if he's wearing boots, either."

"Come on," James said. "We'll tell him about the mud."

They broke into a run and quickly reached the muddy road. Blackie was running beside them.

"Hey!" Mandy called after the boy. "Don't go down there!"

"Come back!" James yelled.

The scruffy little dog following the boy turned and put his head to one side, as if listening to Mandy and James. But the boy just kept walking.

"You'll get stuck!" Mandy called.

"You can't walk through the mud!" James cried. Even Blackie joined in with a couple of woofs, though he didn't know what he was barking at. The scruffy dog stopped and looked around again when he heard Blackie bark, but the boy didn't turn.

"Well!" Mandy said.

"That's rude, don't you think?" said James. "Ignoring us like that. I mean, we're only trying to help."

Mandy shrugged. "Oh, well," she said, "he'll find out for himself soon enough about the mud. What a strange boy. I wonder who he is."

"Maybe he just doesn't want to be friends," said James.

"I think his dog does, though," said Mandy.

James laughed. "That's just the sort of thing you *would* say, Mandy Hope!"

2
Mystery Solved

Mandy didn't think any more about the boy and the dog until the following Monday at school. Mrs. Todd, Mandy's teacher, finished taking attendance and called the class to order.

"I've got some news for you," she said to her class. "There will be a new boy joining us this morning."

Mandy looked around the class. There wasn't anyone new there yet. She hadn't seen anyone new in the playground earlier, either.

"His name is Joey Appleyard," Mrs. Todd said. She glanced at her watch. "I've asked him to join us ten minutes late today because I wanted to speak to you about him first."

The class sat up and listened carefully.

"Our new boy — Joey — is deaf," Mrs. Todd said. "That means we all have to be a little bit more thoughtful and a bit more helpful."

Gary Roberts put up his hand. "Can he talk?" he asked.

Mrs. Todd nodded. "Yes. He can speak perfectly well. He's only been deaf for about two years. He learned to speak in the usual way when he was a baby. His speech sounds a little bit strange now, though, because he can't hear what he's saying. So I don't want any of you to make fun of him."

She looked around the class. "In a few months there'll be a learning assistant here. She'll help Joey understand the instructions that I give. Until then, I think it would be best if he sits at the front of the class. He can face me, at Mandy's table." She smiled at Mandy. "And I know you'll help him as much as possible, won't you, Mandy?"

Mandy nodded, pleased to be asked.

"Now, I want you all to treat Joey just like you treat the rest of your friends," Mrs. Todd went on. "All you've got to remember is to look at him when you're speaking to him so that he can read your lips. Try to speak very clearly, and don't stand behind him and talk, because then he won't be able to read your lips."

She walked over to the classroom door. "I think I see him outside in the corridor now."

The children shifted in their seats, craning their necks, eager to see this new boy.

Mrs. Todd ushered Joey in, and everyone stared at him, feeling just slightly disappointed because he didn't look any different. He looked just like anyone else. He was of average height — just a bit taller than Mandy — with short brown hair and ears that stuck out very slightly.

When she saw him, Mandy gasped in surprise. It was the boy who'd been on Main Street on Saturday. Of course! *That* was why he didn't turn around when they shouted. He hadn't heard them!

"This is Joey," Mrs. Todd said, her hand on Joey's shoulder. She led him over to Mandy's table.

Joey stared at her lips as Mrs. Todd spoke slowly and very precisely. "Joey, this is Mandy. She'll show you around the school at lunchtime and help you if you get stuck with anything."

"Thank you," Joey said. He had a rather loud, harsh voice.

"Hello, Joey," Mandy said slowly and carefully. She felt self-conscious as she spoke, as if she were in a play.

"Hello, Joey," everyone at Mandy's table said, speaking clearly and moving their lips in an exaggerated way.

Sarah Drummond burst out giggling.

"That's enough, Sarah," said Mrs. Todd sharply. "Let's not give Joey a bad first impression of us. We hope he's going to be really happy here." She clapped her hands. "Now, we've got English first thing. Let's get our books out and begin."

By the end of the day, Mandy felt that she and Joey were getting along quite well. Sometimes she forgot what she'd been told and spoke too quickly to him, and often he had to ask her to repeat what she'd said. Once or twice she'd even had to write things down or make signs with her hands. But by and large they seemed to be managing.

Joey was shy, Mandy realized. He hated being stared at and didn't like being the center of attention at all. This made Mandy feel that she wanted to look after him, and she'd tried to stop everyone crowding around him at lunchtime.

"Where do you live?" she asked him as they walked across the playground after school.

"Taggart Lane," Joey said.

Mandy nodded. "It's nice up there. It's near where my grandma and grandpa live."

James was waiting inside the school gates for Mandy. He was a year younger and in the class below Mandy and Joey. Mandy had already introduced the two boys at lunchtime.

"James and I will walk home with you if you like," Mandy said. "I'm going to see my grandma and grandpa anyway."

"Okay," Joey said in his loud, flat voice.

As they came out of the school gates Mandy gave a squeal of delight. "Oh! There's your dog again!" she said. "He's come to meet you."

"What?" Joey said, looking puzzled.

"Sorry," said Mandy, "I forgot to face you. Your dog," she pointed. "He's waiting across the street for you."

Joey's face split into a grin. "But he's not mine," he said.

"We saw him with you on Saturday," James said, careful to face Joey.

Joey nodded. "He's been following me

13

around ever since we moved in last Friday. He even came to school with me this morning."

"Then who owns him?" Mandy asked as the dog ran over to them and leaped up on Joey excitedly. "Where does he live?"

Joey shook his head. "I don't know. He just seems to appear when I come out my front door."

"He's adorable!" Mandy bent to pick up the excited, scruffy little bundle of fur. "I don't know what kind of a dog he is, though. A little terrier and a little spaniel — he's got a little of everything in him, really."

Joey nodded. "I call him Scruff."

"Scruff sounds right," James said, ruffling his fur, "but he's a great dog."

Mandy nodded admiringly. "He's really cute." She put the dog down, and he danced around Joey's feet. "He doesn't have a collar," she went on. "I wonder where he came from. Will you . . . do you think your mom will let you keep him if he doesn't belong to anyone?"

Joey shook his head sadly. "My mom doesn't

like dogs," he said. "I think she's scared of them."

"Oh, that's a pity," Mandy said. She bit her lip. "I suppose I'd better ask my mom and dad if they know anyone who's lost a dog."

"What did you say?" Joey said.

"Sorry," Mandy said. "My mom and dad are vets," she explained slowly and clearly. "We live at the other end of the village, in a place called Animal Ark."

Joey laughed. "Is it really called that?"

James nodded and added, "And there's not an animal around here that Mandy doesn't know about."

Mandy looked at Joey and Scruff playing around together. "You two really get along well," she said. "Wouldn't it be great if we could persuade your mom to —"

"We'd better find out if he belongs to someone first," James said hastily. "Before you start giving out pets."

Mandy laughed. "All right," she said. "First things first."

3

Something Surprising

Mrs. Appleyard, Joey's mom, was standing at their garden gate looking for him. She had an anxious expression on her face. It was clear she was worried about Joey and wondering if he'd had a good day at his new school.

When she saw him coming down the road with Mandy and James, she waved and smiled at them. But then Scruff appeared, and she frowned.

"Shoo!" she said when Scruff ran up to her. "What are you doing here again? Go away!"

Joey, Mandy, and James exchanged glances as Scruff ran down the street. He sat himself on the sidewalk, keeping an eye on Joey from a distance.

Joey introduced Mandy and James to his mother, and they stood and talked with her while Joey went indoors to drop off his backpack.

"Welcome to Welford," James said politely. "I hope you like it."

Mandy nodded agreement. "It's really nice living here," she said. "I'm sure you'll be happy." She was dying to say something about Scruff, but she thought she'd better be careful.

"Mrs. Todd, our teacher, told us all about Joey being deaf," she said. "How we have to look at him when we're talking and things like that."

Mrs. Appleyard nodded. "It's probably going

to be difficult for him at school sometimes," she said. "He'll be getting an assistant soon, though, someone to help when he doesn't catch what Mrs. Todd says."

"Oh, we're helping with that already," Mandy said eagerly. "Joey's in my class, and he's sitting next to me." She smiled. "I'm going to get really good at speaking to him. I have to try to remember to move my lips correctly."

Mrs. Appleyard relaxed a little. "That's nice of you," she said. "Joey had a hard time at his last school, where some of the children weren't so understanding. I'm glad that he's with someone who's looking out for him." She looked worriedly up the road toward Scruff. "But if you really want to help, you could start by keeping that dog away!"

There was silence. James nudged Mandy. Mandy nudged him back. She cleared her throat. "Actually," she said, "Joey really seems to like Scr — . . . that dog. And the dog likes him, too."

"Yes, but even so . . ." Mrs. Appleyard said.

"He was waiting for Joey outside school today," James volunteered.

"Hm . . ." said Mrs. Appleyard.

"He seems like a sweet little dog," Mandy said tentatively.

Mrs. Appleyard tightened her lips. "I don't like dogs," she said.

"Oh, but why not?" Mandy couldn't stop bursting out. "Dogs are *great*. They're really loyal, and they stick with you through thick and thin."

"Yes, well," Mrs. Appleyard said, "I'm afraid you must allow me to disagree with you about that. When I was about Joey's age, I made friends with a little stray dog that seemed as friendly and sweet as this one. But one day it turned on me and bit me. I've never been able to trust a dog since."

"Oh, that's really sad," Mandy said. "Sad because the dog bit you, of course, but also sad because now you don't like *any* dogs."

Mrs. Appleyard smiled suddenly. "I can tell

you're a real animal lover. I bet you've got a dog yourself."

Joey had come outside again now, and he and James began to kick an old tennis ball back and forth. Meanwhile, Mandy explained to Mrs. Appleyard about her mom and dad being vets. "I don't have a dog, though," she finished, "but James lets me share Blackie. He's a Labrador, and I can play with him whenever I like. I also get to see all the animals that come to Animal Ark for treatment."

"Now I know who you are!" Mrs. Appleyard exclaimed. "I've met your grandmother. She came over with some homemade cookies the day we moved in. They were delicious!"

"That sounds like Grandma, all right," Mandy smiled. "She's the best baker in Welford."

The telephone began to ring inside Joey's house, and his mom turned to answer it. "You and James are welcome to come over whenever you like," she said. "And will you tell Joey for me that his snack will be ready in ten minutes. And he's not to encourage that dog!"

Mandy promised to pass on the message. While she was talking to Joey and James, the ball they were playing with rolled into the gutter and went farther down the road.

No one paid much attention to the ball or Scruff going to get it until he was standing behind Joey with the ball in his mouth. He put it down and began to bark to attract Joey's attention. Joey, who was busy watching Mandy's lips as she was talking, still didn't realize Scruff was there.

Scruff barked on, but before Mandy or James could tell Joey about him, the little dog suddenly put out a paw and tapped Joey's foot.

Joey looked down, surprised. "Scruff!" he said. "What do you want?"

Mandy touched Joey's arm to catch his attention. "He's brought the ball back," she said.

Joey saw it and bent and ruffled the dog's fur. "Good boy!" he said. He picked up the ball. "You're a good dog, aren't you?"

A sudden thought occurred to Mandy. Startled, she looked at James, who had the same surprised expression on his face.

"Hey," he said. "Do you think what I think?"

Mandy nodded violently. "Yes!" she said.

Joey was looking at them, puzzled. "What's going on?" he asked.

"Well," Mandy said, "I don't know how he *does* know, but I think Scruff knows that you can't hear. He started off by barking at you, and when you didn't pay any attention, he put his paw on your foot."

"Wow!" Joey said. "That's fantastic!"

"*What* a smart dog!" Mandy said.

There was a knocking from the window of Joey's house, and Mandy and James looked around. Joey followed their glance.

"Snack time!" Joey's mom mouthed. She made gestures of eating, and then she beckoned Joey in.

Joey looked down at Scruff sitting patiently at his feet, then at Mandy.

"What are you going to do about Scruff?"

Mandy asked. "Your mom said not to encourage him."

Joey bit his lip, then he grinned. "I might forget that!" he said, and all three of them laughed.

Mandy and James said good-bye and told Joey they'd see him the next day.

As James and Mandy walked down the road, James looked back. "Hey," he said, "look at Scruff!"

As they watched, Scruff squeezed under Joey's garden gate and settled himself down in the long grass by the front wall.

"I don't think Mrs. Appleyard is going to get rid of Scruff very easily," James said.

"Neither do I," said Mandy. "I think Scruff's already made up his mind where he wants to live!"

4

Biscuits and Bones

Mandy was deep in thought when she arrived at Lilac Cottage, where her grandma and grandpa lived. Mostly she was thinking about Scruff and Joey and what she could do to persuade Mrs. Appleyard to give the little dog a chance.

When Mandy went around to the back of

the cottage, Grandpa was in the garden picking pole beans. A basketful of them stood on the grass next to him.

"I hope you still like beans!" Grandpa said, peering through a screen of tall bean plants. "I'm doing a last picking, and I believe I've still got enough to supply twelve grocery stores. However fast I pick them, they just seem to keep on growing."

"I *love* pole beans!" Mandy said. "And you know Dad does. We'll eat as many as you want to give us."

"Good!" Grandpa said. He threw some more beans in the basket and then straightened up. "I'm glad you've come by, Mandy. I've been looking for an excuse to have a break."

He picked up the basket of beans, and they went inside the cottage. "You know your grandma," he went on. "She's a real slave driver. Once I start work in that garden, I'm not allowed to stop without a good reason."

"Oh, stop kidding!" Mandy said, giggling. Grandma was pouring boiling water from

the kettle into her cup. She got Mandy a cold drink out of the refrigerator.

"What's new?" she asked. "You look as if you have something to tell me."

"I do!" Mandy said, giving her a hug. "There's a new boy at school, and he's sitting next to me because he's deaf, and I've got to look after him and tell him things. I have to speak to him very care-ful-ly and prop-er-ly," she said, separating each of her words into syllables.

Grandma smiled. "Well," she said, "it may interest you to know that I've already met your new friend. *And* his mom."

"Oh, of course you have!" Mandy exclaimed. "Mrs. Appleyard said you came by with some cookies."

"She's a very nice woman," Grandma said, stirring sugar into Grandpa's tea. "She told me that she's a widow, and she's brought up Joey on her own. He seems like a very nice boy, too."

"You said his mom seemed a little overanxious about him," Grandpa added.

"With good cause!" Grandma said. "He was very seriously ill, you see," she explained to Mandy. "One of the effects of his illness was that he lost his hearing. He had to have months off from school, and then when he went back some of the children gave him a hard time. They teased him about the way he spoke."

"I don't really understand why he speaks in such a funny way," Mandy said. "Sometimes he just yells out things and makes me jump!"

"Well, it's something to do with not being able to hear yourself," Grandma said. "You forget how to adjust the tone you're speaking in, so you can't tell if you're shouting or not. And you forget how to pronounce certain words, too. And new words are difficult."

"Poor boy," Grandpa said.

"There's something else," Mandy said. "There's a dog that's been hanging around Joey ever since they moved in."

"I saw it!" Grandma said. "Cute little thing. It was sitting in the front garden when I stopped by. Mrs. Appleyard chased it away."

"That's just it," Mandy said. "Mrs. Appleyard doesn't like dogs. She got bitten by one when she was young."

"Well, not everyone's crazy about animals like you are!" Grandpa said.

"But this dog seems really good to Joey," Mandy went on. "He's never had a pet before, and he really likes Scruff, too."

"Scruff, is it?" Grandpa said. "So you've named him already."

Mandy smiled. "Joey did. It's a sweet little dog . . . and we think it's already figured out that Joey's deaf." She explained how Scruff had brought back the tennis ball and used his paw to get Joey's attention.

"Well, I never!" Grandma said.

"Did you know that there are special dogs trained to do that?" Grandpa said. "A man I knew years back named George had one. It wasn't a special pedigree or anything, just your average mixed breed. The dog would let him know when there was someone at the door, and so on. Hearing dogs, they call them."

Mandy put down her glass. "I've heard of guide dogs for the blind," she said, "but I didn't know they had special dogs for the deaf as well. What else did George's dog do?"

"Well," Grandpa said, "it's a few years ago now, but if I remember, he did things around the house. He would let George know if someone was at the door or if the telephone was ringing."

"But then what would happen?" Grandma asked. "George couldn't hear who was speaking, could he?"

"I think he had a special amplifier on his telephone that made people sound ten times as loud as they really were. Mind you, he wasn't completely deaf. George had *some* hearing."

Mandy frowned. "I'm not sure whether Joey has or not. But how did George's dog tell him that someone wanted him?" she asked.

"He used to go up and put his paw on

George's knee. That was the signal that something was up. When George was alerted, his dog would take him to where the noise was coming from. He'd lead him along to the front door or the telephone or whatever."

"I see," Mandy said. She sat for a moment, deep in thought. Then she said, "Do you think James and I might be able to train Scruff to help Joey?"

"To have the same hearing-dog skills as George's dog?" Grandpa asked. He shook his head doubtfully. "I wouldn't know, honey."

"I don't think you'd have time to train a dog that well," Grandma said. "I mean, look at the amount of time you and James have spent on Blackie, and he's still not exactly top of the class in obedience, is he?"

Mandy smiled wryly. "Sometimes I think Blackie enjoys being difficult. He *likes* disobeying us," she said. "But Scruff's already got a head start. So if we could only teach him a little more, then Mrs. Appleyard might let him stay."

"You'd better see what your mom and dad have to say about it first," Grandma said.

Mandy's eyes sparkled. "But wouldn't it be great if we could teach Scruff to let Joey know when someone wants him? Like when there's someone at the front door?"

Grandma and Grandpa agreed that it would. "But don't get too attached to the idea," Grandma said. "You might not be able to talk Mrs. Appleyard into letting Joey keep him."

Grandpa, who'd been dividing the pole beans up into piles, suddenly asked, "Does Joey like pole beans?"

"Now, how do you expect Mandy to know that?" Grandma said.

"Well, if you *think* he does," Grandpa went on, "you could take some over to him on your way home. I've had enough beans this year to feed all of Welford!"

Mandy laughed. "I'll certainly take him some, then."

A little later, with two packages of pole beans wrapped in newspaper under her arm,

Mandy set off for home. She was going to stop by Joey's house on the way.

Grandpa had started work in the garden again, and Mandy paused to talk to him. "I'm worried about Scruff," she said. "I think he's sleeping in Joey's front yard, and I don't know what he's doing for food. I didn't want to ask Joey about it in front of his mom."

Grandpa scratched his head. "I don't know what to say, Mandy," he said. "It's difficult. If Mrs. Appleyard doesn't want the dog there, maybe you shouldn't be encouraging him."

"I know," Mandy sighed. "But he *is* there, and he's probably hungry."

Grandpa thought for a moment. "You're going to Joey's with the pole beans, aren't you? So how about taking a couple of handfuls of dog biscuits with you?"

"That's a good idea," Mandy said.

"There are some in the shed, left from when you were trying to train Blackie in our garden."

Mandy brightened up. "And I could just accidentally drop them in Joey's front yard, couldn't I?"

Grandpa winked. "But if anyone sees you, don't tell them where you got them!"

As Mandy went through Joey's front gate, Scruff came out from his hiding place in the long grass inside the wall. The little dog jumped at her, pleased to see her.

"Hello, boy!" Mandy said. She bent down to pet him, then straightened up and looked around carefully to make sure no one was watching. "How about a few dog biscuits?" she asked softly, and she took them out of her pocket and put them in a pile on the grass.

When Scruff started crunching them, Mandy reached up to ring Joey's front doorbell, just as Joey opened the door.

They both laughed, startled to see each other.

"I've come by with some beans from my grandpa," Mandy said, and she handed over the newspaper bundle.

Joey thanked her. Then, from under his sweater, he drew out a bone. "I was just coming out to give this to Scruff," he said.

Mandy smiled, relieved. "I *thought* you'd be feeding him. He's living in your front yard, isn't he? James and I saw him going under the gate as we left."

Joey nodded. "I've been managing to save him something from most meals." He glanced toward the house. "I don't know whether my mom knows or not. If she does, she's not saying anything about it — and neither am I!"

Mandy smiled. "All three of us — you, James, and I — will have to try to get her to change her mind about dogs."

"That would be great!" said Joey. "I'd *love* it if Scruff were mine."

5

Mixed Feelings

"Jean, guess what!" Mandy said, bursting into the waiting room of Animal Ark.

Jean Knox, the receptionist, looked up from the papers she was working on. "Don't tell me," she said. "It's something about an animal, right?"

Mandy looked surprised. "How did you know?"

Jean smiled. "Because it's usually something about an animal with you."

"Well, it's not just about an animal," Mandy began. She started to tell her about Joey. When she got to the part about Mrs. Appleyard not liking dogs, she heard a voice saying, "Oh, dear me, no!"

Mandy stopped, astonished.

"Oh, dear me, no . . ." the strange voice said again and added, "poor Polly!"

As Mandy looked around, Jean burst out laughing and pointed up at the shelf. "Meet Polly," she said.

"A parrot!" Mandy said, looking up, amazed.

It was a parrot. A beautiful big one, with bright yellow breast feathers and striking blue-and-red wing feathers.

"Where did *she* come from?" Mandy asked in awe. She hadn't seen a parrot that closely before and certainly had never heard one speaking so clearly.

"A man brought her in," Jean said. "She's losing her feathers. Look at her chest."

Mandy looked closer and saw there was pink, scrawny-looking skin showing through the parrot's thinning chest feathers. "Poor thing!" she said.

"She's in for observation and a few nights' stay," Jean went on. "Her owner says she likes being around people, so we're keeping her here."

"Good idea," Mandy said. "She can see everything that's going on." She went behind the desk and was about to put her finger through the bars of the cage to stroke Polly when the bird made a sudden movement toward her. Mandy jerked her finger back quickly.

"No, don't take any chances," Jean said. "Her owner says she's very friendly, but you never know with birds. She might be feeling out of sorts and take a quick peck of a nice pink finger."

"Does she speak much?" Mandy asked.

"When she wants to," Jean said. She pursed her lips. "And when she does, she comes out with a few things that your teacher might not approve of!"

Mandy laughed. She was about to ask if Jean knew of anyone who'd lost a dog like Scruff, when her mother poked her head through the door.

"Mandy! I thought I heard you," she said. "Did you have a good day at school?"

Mandy nodded, her eyes shining. "Lots to tell you, Mom," she said.

"That's good," said Dr. Emily Hope. "Come quickly. Dinner's ready. I have my yoga class tonight, so we don't have much time."

Mandy picked up her backpack. "Bye, Jean. Bye, Polly," she said. She stood by the bird's cage and said "Good–bye, Polly" twice more, but the parrot didn't reply.

"As I was saying," Jean said, "she speaks when she wants to."

Mandy sat in the dining room with her mom and dad. As she ate her dinner, she wondered how to bring up the subject of Scruff. Her feelings about the dog were mixed. On the one hand she knew that if someone who loved Scruff had lost him, it would be wonderful to reunite them. On the other hand, now that Joey had gotten so fond of Scruff, it would be *terrible* for Joey to lose him.

"You know, I've just been telling you about the new boy, Joey," she said after some thought. "Well, there's a nice little dog that's been hanging around him, wanting to be friends."

Her mother and father laughed. "Whenever you take an interest in something, there's sure to be an animal lurking somewhere in the background!" Dr. Emily said.

"That's just it," Mandy said, "he *is* in the background. Joey's mom won't let him in the house."

Dr. Adam Hope finished his meal and put his plate to one side. "Why don't you tell us all about it," he said.

So Mandy did, finishing with the story about Grandpa's friend with the hearing dog.

"So I was thinking," she said, "that if Mrs.

Appleyard would let Joey keep Scruff, then maybe James and I could teach him some of the things that a real hearing dog would do." She looked from her mom to her dad and back again. "What do you think?"

Dr. Emily and Dr. Adam thought about the question a long moment. Mandy's mother said, "I really don't think that would be possible, darling. You see, those dogs receive months of specialized training."

"Yes, but Scruff's already shown he can do it," Mandy said. "He seemed to realize all on his own that barking at Joey got no response."

"Well, that's true," her mother said. "If it wasn't just coincidence, of course."

"Well, if he's made a start for himself, I can't see that it would do any harm trying," Dr. Adam said. "Though I really don't think you should expect too much, Mandy. And you should try not to be disappointed if it doesn't work out."

"When would you do all this?" Mandy's mother asked. "Training like that takes a good deal of time, and I wouldn't want you to fall behind with your homework."

"Vacation is coming up," Mandy said. "James and I could go over every day and work with Scruff and Joey then. It would be our project for the week. A doggy dare!"

"Well," Dr. Adam said, "I suppose you could try, but only if Mrs. Appleyard agrees."

Dr. Emily nodded. "One other thing, darling," she said. "Whose dog *is* he? He must belong to someone."

Mandy shrugged. "I haven't seen him around here before, not ever. And I haven't seen any flyers."

"Well," said Dr. Emily, "before you get too excited about him helping Joey, perhaps you ought to put up some flyers of your own."

"To advertise Scruff?" Mandy asked.

Her mother nodded. "To ask if anyone's lost a dog of that description."

"But suppose they *have*?" Mandy asked plaintively.

"Well," said Dr. Emily gently, "it would be

best to find that out before you've trained Scruff, wouldn't it? Before you all get too fond of him. And wouldn't it feel good to reunite him with his real owner?"

"I suppose so," Mandy said a bit glumly, wondering how Joey would feel about that.

"Another thing . . ." Dr. Emily said. "You really should be careful with a strange dog that no one knows anything about."

"I was just going to say that," said Mandy's father.

"I know it's not nice to think about, but he could have something wrong with him, some disease or other," Dr. Emily went on. "You wouldn't want him to pass it on to all the dogs in the neighborhood, would you?"

Mandy shook her head slowly.

Her mother stood up and began collecting the plates. "I'm off to yoga," she said. "Do I have two volunteers to do the dishes?"

Mandy jumped up. "Of course you have, Mom," she said. She didn't mind doing the dishes — and anyway, she wanted to get her father on his own.

"You know how you and Mom were saying how important it is to check out Scruff's health?" she began as they were putting away the plates and silverware.

Her father looked at her quizzically. "I don't remember saying *that*."

"Well, you both said we shouldn't get too fond of a dog that we don't know anything about, didn't you?"

"Mmm," said Dr. Adam. He looked at Mandy with his head to one side. "Somehow, I think I know what's coming."

"Well, do you think you could check him out for us?" Mandy asked. "Give him the green light? Oh, please say you will!"

Dr. Adam pretended to look doubtful. "I don't know about that," he said. "Who would pay for this checkup?"

Mandy bit her lip worriedly. "If you could let us have a special rate, I . . ."

Dr. Adam began laughing. "I was only teasing you," he said. "Of course I'll check the dog out. When do you want to bring him in?"

James came by after dinner. Mandy told him about Grandpa's pal with the hearing dog and filled him in on her father's promise to check Scruff's health.

"In the meantime, though, I said we'd make some flyers," Mandy said. "Mom and Dad both say that we need to make sure that Scruff hasn't already got a home."

"I can help with those," James said. "We could do them on my computer. I can make posters and invitations and all kinds of stuff on it."

"That would be great," Mandy said. "And we have four days before vacation, so we can put a flyer on the bulletin board at school, too."

The school bulletin board was where everyone put up news items or things they had for sale; if you had some books to sell or an animal that needed looking after during vacations, this was the best place to let people know. Some time back, James had put up a notice saying that he wanted a puppy, and Mandy had seen it and told him about Blackie. That was how they'd started to become best friends.

"You could do the signs and print them out," Mandy said, "and I'll ask Dad if I can borrow his instant camera and get some photos of Scruff to paste on them."

James nodded. "The funny thing is," he said, pushing his glasses back on his nose, "we don't want the signs to *work*, do we?"

"What do you mean?" Mandy asked.

"Well," James said, "we really don't want to find Scruff's owners, do we?"

Mandy shook her head. "Not really."

James grinned. "This must be the only time anyone's advertised anything and hoped no one would reply!"

6

A Wonderful Trick

"Is he okay?" James asked anxiously, as Mandy came out of Animal Ark clinic with Scruff in her arms.

"He's fine!" Mandy said. "Dad gave him a checkup and said he's a fit little dog. He's a bit underweight, but Dad said he'd soon make that up."

"That's good!" James said.

"And guess what? Dad gave him all his shots, too. And his worm pills and everything!"

"So he's fit and ready to go?"

"That's right," Mandy said.

Once outside, Mandy put Scruff down on the sidewalk and gave him a pat.

"All we need to do now is figure out whether he can help Joey —" she began.

"— and persuade Joey's mom to take him in!" James finished.

They began to walk along the road together, Scruff running in front of them. It was the first day of vacation, and they were going to meet Joey on the village green. The three of them were going to start trying to train Scruff.

That morning, Mandy had woken up early and gone to get Scruff, who was still living in Joey's front yard.

Mrs. Appleyard was pretending that Scruff didn't exist. Mandy wondered if she was secretly hoping that Scruff's real owners would turn up and claim him.

"Has anyone come into Animal Ark about our flyers?" James asked.

"No one," Mandy said. "We put up four, didn't we? One at school, one on the green, one outside the general store, and one at Animal Ark, and there hasn't been a single reply. No one's even said they've ever *seen* him before."

"Good," James said with satisfaction.

They neared the village green, chatting all the way. When they turned the corner, they saw Joey standing under the oak tree.

"Scruff, there's Joey!" Mandy said. The dog looked up at her curiously. "It's Joey! Off you go, boy!"

Hearing the word "Joey" the dog pricked up his ears. He looked around and then glanced ahead and recognized his friend. He gave a short yelp and began to run down the road as fast as his little legs would carry him.

"Look at him go!" James cried.

"He really loves Joey, doesn't he?" Mandy said.

James nodded. "It will be a real shame if Joey isn't able to keep him."

Mandy squeezed James's arm. "It's up to us, then, to see that he's allowed to stay."

Joey was smiling from ear to ear when they reached him.

"Scruff knows me, doesn't he?" he boomed.

Mandy nodded. "Of course he does," she said, speaking slowly and clearly.

"And is he all right? Did your dad say he's healthy?"

"He's absolutely fine," Mandy said. "Nothing to worry about at all. Dad's given him all the shots he needs, too."

"Great!" Joey said. He looked at James. "Why didn't you bring Blackie with you?"

James shook his head, and his floppy hair fell into his eyes. "I thought I'd better not," he said, speaking as clearly as Mandy had done. "One dog at a time is best for training."

Mandy nodded in agreement. "How we want Scruff to behave is different from how we want Blackie to behave. Blackie would get all confused."

"And he's bad enough now!" James said with a laugh.

"Okay," Mandy said. "We'll start with the easiest thing — what we think Scruff knows already."

Mandy had spoken to her mom and dad several times about Scruff's training. They had emphasized that Mandy and James should begin very slowly, repeat everything over and over again, and not try to do too much at once.

"You'll confuse Scruff if you do," her dad had told her.

"If he does get it right, though, be ready with lots of praise and encouragement," her mom had added.

"So," James asked now, "you mean we should call to Joey and get Scruff to tell him we're calling?"

Mandy nodded and turned to face Joey. "You walk away with Scruff," she said, "and when you're crossing the green, James and I will call you. Don't turn around, though, even if you think we're calling. We'll see if Scruff does anything."

Joey beamed. "Sounds like fun," he said. If it meant that his mom might be persuaded to let him keep Scruff, then it would be fantastic.

Joey and Scruff set off. "Bye, you two!" he said, just for effect. Mandy and James called, "See you!" and "Good-bye!"

They let Joey get halfway across the green and then shouted, "Hey, Joey!" and "Come back here!"

Joey continued walking, although Scruff looked around at them once or twice.

"Come back!" Mandy called at the top of her voice.

"Joey! Joey!" James shouted.

But Joey kept on walking. Scruff looked around again and then looked up at Joey. Seeing that his master didn't seem worried, the little dog trotted on.

Joey got all the way to the other side of the green, then he turned, waved to Mandy and

James, and shrugged. Mandy beckoned him to come back.

He looked disappointed when he reached them. "It didn't work," he said.

"Never mind," Mandy said. "We didn't really expect it to work that quickly. We'll try again."

They tried again, as before, except this time they shouted even louder; they *yelled* for Joey to come back. Scruff looked back at them again but still didn't do anything to alert Joey.

The next time, when Scruff heard the children calling, he actually looked up at Joey and gave a couple of barks, but of course Joey didn't hear him.

After two more tries, Joey was getting a bit downhearted. "That time outside my house, maybe he didn't really tell me that the ball was there," Joey said. "Maybe it was just coincidence."

Mandy shook her head. She was disappointed, too, although she wasn't going to show it. "I'm sure it wasn't," she said. "I'm *sure* he knows. He's just thinking about something else."

"We've got to keep trying!" said James.

The next time Joey set off and they started shouting for him to come back, Mrs. Ponsonby, the snobbish woman who lived in Bleakfell Hall, walked past.

"Well, really, children!" she said. "Such shouting and screaming! Is it really necessary to make such a racket?"

"Sorry," Mandy said. "It's just . . ." She was about to explain, when Mrs. Ponsonby waved dismissively. "Children today. Really!" she said. She shook her head and walked on.

James and Mandy rolled their eyes at each other. They didn't dare make another sound until Mrs. Ponsonby had disappeared into the general store. By then, Joey had reached the other side of the green and had to be motioned back.

"Sorry," Mandy said when he arrived. "We didn't do that one correctly. Let's try again."

The next time they increased their efforts, yelling Joey's name, waving their arms, and jumping about like mad. And this time it actually worked! *This* time Scruff looked up at Joey and barked. Then, getting no response, he jumped up, licked his hand, then pawed at his foot.

When Joey looked down at Scruff, the dog ran a few steps backward, toward Mandy and James, then stopped and looked up at Joey as if to say, "Look! Someone wants you!"

"Oh!" Joey said, pretending surprise. "I'd better go back." And he turned to go back to Mandy and James.

When he reached them, they all jumped around, really excited. "It worked!" Mandy said.

"He did it!" shouted James.

"Good old Scruff!" said Joey. And Scruff ran around and around in circles barking, not knowing what all the fuss was about but happy to be part of it.

They made Scruff repeat his behavior three times to make sure it wasn't a fluke. Now that he'd got the idea of what was wanted, he was able to do it without all the yelling and waving. It only took one or two calls of "Hey, Joey!" for him to pat Joey's foot with his paw or jump up and put his nose in Joey's hand.

Once they'd got that down, James said they should make sure that it would work in other places, not just on the green.

"I mean, how many times is Joey going to walk across there?" he said.

So they varied it by having Joey walk toward the general store and then did it again across the street. Soon after, Mandy's grandpa came by on his way to church bell-ringing practice, and they asked *him* to call Joey.

"We just want to make sure that Scruff will tell Joey when other people call him, not just us," Mandy explained, and everyone was thrilled when he did so.

When they'd covered just about every combination they could think of, and Scruff had eaten his way through a whole packet of doggy treats as a reward, the three friends and Scruff made their way to Joey's house.

They stood on the front step, made Scruff look as *un*scruffy as possible, and rang the doorbell.

Mrs. Appleyard greeted them warmly. Then she saw Scruff and sighed. "Is he still around?" she asked. "I was hoping he might disappear."

Mandy cleared her throat. "There's something we want to show you," she said.

"Oh, yes?" Mrs. Appleyard said warily.

Mandy turned to face Joey. "Bye, Joey!" she said. "Good-bye!"

"Bye, Joey!" called James.

"What's going on? Where's he going?" Mrs. Appleyard asked. "His lunch is ready."

"He's not going anywhere," Mandy said, smiling broadly. "But say good-bye anyway."

Mystified, Mrs. Appleyard said good-bye as Joey, accompanied by Scruff, pushed open the gate and shut it behind him. He began to walk down the road.

"Now call him back," Mandy said to Mrs. Appleyard.

Mrs. Appleyard looked more mystified, even a little annoyed. "Don't be silly," she said. "He can't hear me."

"Just try it," Mandy pleaded, "and come to the gate to see what happens."

Mrs. Appleyard walked down to the gate. She called her son's name rather halfheartedly and then gave a squeal of surprise when Scruff immediately jumped up and nudged Joey's hand with his nose. Joey turned, waved to his mom, and came back.

"I don't believe it!" Mrs. Appleyard said.

"Do you want him to do it again?" James asked.

"Well, I . . . yes, I do," said Mrs. Appleyard. Scruff and Joey walked in the other direction and repeated the trick.

When they came back, Mrs. Appleyard stood for some time, shaking her head in disbelief.

"We think we might be able to teach Scruff other things to help Joey, too," Mandy said.

"So can we keep him?" Joey suddenly burst out. "Oh, *please*, Mom. He'll be no trouble. He's such a good dog. He's so smart!"

"My dad's examined him, and he's very healthy!" Mandy said persuasively.

"Well . . ." Mrs. Appleyard began.

"Oh, please say yes," James pleaded. "Joey and Scruff really love each other."

"And Scruff would be so good for him . . ." Mandy added.

Mrs. Appleyard sighed and smiled. "I know when I'm beaten," she said, "and I must admit that what that dog's just done is pretty amazing. He can stay for the moment, but he's on two weeks' trial. If he shows any signs of being ag-gressive during that time, if there's any biting or snarling or chewing of the furniture, then he'll have to go. Okay?"

Joey flung his arms around his mom. "Thanks, Mom!" he said, "Oh, thanks so much!"

And as Mandy and James walked away, they felt *very* pleased with themselves.

7

Training Troubles

"How's the dog training going?" Grandpa asked a couple of days later. He'd come to Animal Ark to leave another bundle of beans. "Are you making much progress?"

"Scruff's doing really well," Mandy said happily. "We haven't tried to teach him anything else yet, though. We've just been reworking what you saw him doing on Monday. We thought we'd better go over and over that lesson first."

Grandpa nodded. "Good idea," he said. "You don't want to confuse the poor thing."

"Scruff is on two weeks' trial at the moment," Mandy went on, "so we shouldn't push him too much."

"Is Joey's mom still unsure about having a dog?" Grandpa asked.

Mandy shook her head. "I think she's scared of Scruff. She doesn't say so, but I'm sure she is."

"Well," Grandpa said, "you know what they say. Once bitten, twice shy."

"No, no, no!" came a sudden loud cry from the other side of the door.

"What's *that*?" Grandpa asked, startled.

Mandy laughed. "That's Polly," she said. "A parrot. Jean's got her in reception with her because Polly likes company. She's in for observation, because her feathers are dropping out."

"Oh, my!" Grandpa said. "A talking parrot, eh? Very clever, some birds!"

"And some animals!" Mandy said promptly. "*Especially* hearing dogs."

"That's true," Grandpa said. "George's dog made a world of difference to him."

Mandy beamed. "And Scruff is going to make a world of difference to Joey!"

"Scruff's only allowed downstairs," Joey said. "Mom won't let me have him in my bedroom. He has to sleep in the kitchen in a cardboard box."

"But it's a nice *big* cardboard box," Mandy said, "and at least he's indoors! That's a start."

Mandy and James were in Joey's house. Joey's mother had gone into Walton, the nearby town, to do some shopping. Mandy, James, and Joey were taking the opportunity to give Scruff some training.

Mandy stared down at Scruff, who was wagging his tail as if he knew he was about to learn something new and was looking forward to it. "Now, how shall we organize his next lesson?"

"What are we going to teach him next?" Joey asked.

"To tell you when the front doorbell is ringing, I think," Mandy said.

"Would it be best if we showed Scruff how it *should* be done first?" James asked.

Mandy nodded. "That's a good idea," she said. "Otherwise he won't know how things are supposed to go."

"So . . ." James said slowly, figuring it out in his head, "I'll go outside and ring the doorbell. You sit in here with Joey, and when you hear the bell, you get up to answer it."

"Okay," Mandy said.

She and Joey sat down in the living room with a book each. Scruff sat at Joey's feet. James went outside, and a moment later the doorbell rang.

"Oh, I hear the bell," Mandy said for Scruff's benefit. "I'd better go and answer it."

She got up, went to the door, and let James in.

Next it was James's turn to sit with Joey while Mandy went outside, and the whole thing was repeated.

When they were all back in the living room, Mandy perched on the arm of the sofa. "What did Scruff do when I rang? Did he look up at all?" she asked.

James nodded. "He looked up, and he gave a little bark. Nothing else."

Mandy bent down to ruffle his fur. "Now let's try *not* answering the door and see what he does."

They tried this, with James going outside first. This time, when she heard James ringing the bell, Mandy didn't move. She stayed exactly where she was, pretending to read.

Scruff pricked up his ears. Then he looked at both Mandy and Joey and gave a short *wuff*. As the two humans didn't seem bothered by the ringing of the doorbell, though, neither did he. He yawned and put his head on his paws.

James rang again. And again and again. In the end, Mandy went to let him in.

"That doesn't seem to be working," Mandy said. "Scruff just doesn't seem to know what to do."

"Well," James said, "it's an awful lot for him to think about, isn't it? And it did take him a long time on the green before he got it right."

"But he learned in the end!" Joey put in.

"Of course he did," said Mandy.

"I think we ought to go back to basics for a while," James said. "Let's show Scruff a few more times that when the bell rings, someone has to go and answer it."

Mandy and Joey thought this was the best thing, too, so James went outside and rang the bell again. Mandy made a big thing of hearing it this time, saying to Joey and Scruff, "There's someone at the front door!" Then Mandy, Joey, and Scruff all went to answer it together.

They did this three times. Then James went outside again and rang the bell, and Mandy just sat there, not saying a word. She looked hard at Scruff, urging him to move. Apart from pricking up his ears, though, he didn't budge. The doorbell had rung so often that he'd even stopped *wuffing* at it.

Finally, Mandy went to let James in. They talked while enjoying the orange juice and cookies that Mrs. Appleyard had left for them.

"Maybe," Mandy said, remembering to face Joey, "Scruff won't do it while *we're* here — you and me, James. Maybe he knows that if the door really needs answering, one of us will do it."

James nodded. "That makes sense," he said.

Joey nodded, too. "Let's try it with me sitting on my own."

Mandy finished her orange juice. "Yes," she said, "let's give that a try."

This time, James took his book into the kitchen, while Mandy went outside. Joey and Scruff stayed in the living room.

Mandy stood on the front doorstep and rang the bell loud and long. Nothing happened. She waited a moment and rang again. And again. Still nothing happened.

She was just about to ring once more when, farther up the road, she spotted her mother coming out of a house. She was carrying her big leather vet's bag.

Mandy ran toward her, waving. "Mom! What are you doing here?"

Her mother smiled. "I've delivered four kittens," she said. "Two black, one white, and one tabby."

"You had to deliver them?" Mandy asked. "I thought cats always did that for themselves."

"They do usually," her mother said, "but this time the first one got stuck. Luckily I managed to turn it around in time with no harm done."

"Four kittens!" Mandy said. "May I go see them?"

"You wouldn't want to see them at the moment," her mother said. "They don't look very pretty. More like little rats."

"I like little rats!" said Mandy.

Her mother laughed. "I know you do," she said, "and I'm sure Mrs. Cobbold will let you see them later, when their eyes are open."

She opened her car door. "How's your dog training session going?"

"Oh!" Mandy said. "I forgot! I'm supposed to be on doorbell duty. Joey and James will wonder what's happened to me."

"Off you go, then, darling," her mother said. "See you at lunchtime."

She waved and drove off, and Mandy walked back to Joey's house in time to see an indignant Mrs. Ponsonby coming down Joey's path.

"I've rung and rung that bell," she said to Mandy, "but no one's answering. There's someone in there, though! I can see them through the window."

"Oh, Mrs. Ponsonby, hang on!" Mandy began.

"I really *can't* hang on," the woman said. "I haven't got all day. I stopped by to welcome our newcomers to Welford, but if they . . ."

"Hello. May I help?" Mrs. Appleyard opened the gate carrying three bulging grocery bags. "Is there something wrong?"

"Well," Mrs. Ponsonby said, "if you call not

answering the door when someone's at home *wrong*, then there is!"

Mrs. Appleyard looked confused. "The children are inside playing, so I can't think . . ." she began.

"I can explain," Mandy said. "We're training Scruff."

Mrs. Ponsonby frowned. "It was you and two other children who were making such a racket on the green on Monday, wasn't it? Shrieking and shouting and carrying on . . ."

Mrs. Appleyard put the bags of shopping down. "Is this true, Mandy? And was Joey involved?"

"Yes, but . . ."

"I mean, *why* are they just sitting in there and not answering the doorbell?" Mrs. Ponsonby began again. "I find it very rude!"

"Mrs. Ponsonby!" Mandy said in a rush. "We're trying to train Scruff, Joey's dog. Joey can't hear, you see, so we want to train Scruff to answer the door."

Mrs. Ponsonby frowned. "This all sounds *most* peculiar."

"And they thought it was *me* outside ringing the bell, so they didn't answer it, and . . ."

"I think I see," Mrs. Appleyard said. She put her key in the lock. "Please come in," she said to Mrs. Ponsonby. "We can introduce ourselves properly, and you can meet Joey."

Mrs. Ponsonby looked at her watch. "I'm afraid I haven't got time now," she said, frowning slightly. "Some other morning, perhaps."

"Oh, but . . ." Mrs. Appleyard began.

"Good day to you both!" Mrs. Ponsonby said, and with a wave of her hand, she was gone.

"Oh, dear," Mandy said to Mrs. Appleyard. "Sorry."

Mrs. Appleyard sighed. "Not a very good way to meet the neighbors, was it? And it was all that dog's fault!"

8

Bad News

"Pretty Polly, pretty Polly," Mandy said encouragingly to the parrot, whose cage was now on the reception desk. "That bird!" she said. "She never speaks when you want her to. She'll wait until I'm right in the middle of an important telephone conversation and then start squawking at the top of her lungs."

Mandy giggled.

"She's going home today, anyway," Jean went on, "and I can't say I'm sorry."

"Did Mom and Dad find out what was wrong with her?"

Jean nodded. "It was mites under her feathers. Your dad has given her a shot and some insect powder."

"Poor Polly!" Mandy said.

"It's lucky she didn't turn out to be *bald* Polly," Jean said. She closed the appointment book she'd been writing in. "How's your vacation going, Mandy? How's Scruff's training program coming along?"

"Not *too* bad," Mandy said cautiously.

The day after the incident with Mrs. Ponsonby, Mandy and Joey and James had tried the front doorbell trick again. After half an hour's hard work they thought that Scruff had almost got the idea. Then Mrs. Appleyard, irritated by the constant ringing of the doorbell, had put a stop to the lessons. They were going to try again that afternoon.

The door from the street opened just then, and a man came in to deliver a package. He was about to go out again when his eye caught a glimpse of the sign on the bulletin board.

"I recognize that dog!" he said suddenly, pointing at Scruff's picture.

Mandy's heart jolted. She stared at the man in horror.

"That's the Browns' dog!" he went on.

Jean shot a sympathetic glance at Mandy. "The Browns' dog?" she asked. "Are they a local family?"

"They live near Walton. They rent the house next to the garage."

"Are you sure?" Mandy asked him.

"Sure as eggs are eggs. I know the dog, see, because I've got one that looks pretty much the same. I take my car into that garage sometimes, and I've seen him on the doorstep or sitting in the front yard."

"Oh," Mandy said, dismayed.

FOUND
MONGREL DOG
MEDIUM SIZED
FLUFFY AND SCRUFFY
PLEASE apply
ANIM
L ARK

"But do you know if they've actually *lost* a dog?" Jean asked.

"I don't know," the man said. "I haven't been over that way for a couple of months. I'm sure it belongs to them, though." He pushed open the door. "Expect they'll be pleased to get it back!"

Mandy swallowed hard.

"Yes. I'm . . . er . . . sure they will," Jean said. "We'll make some inquiries right away."

"Glad to help!" said the man cheerfully as he went out. "I know what it's like when you lose a pet."

As the door shut behind him, Mandy and Jean looked at each other.

"Oh, dear," Jean said sympathetically.

Mandy's eyes filled with tears. "Poor Joey," she said. "And poor Scruff." She bit her lip, "Do you think we can . . ."

Jean shook her head. "Of course not," she said. "Don't even think about it." She patted Mandy's hand. "There may be someone in that Brown family who loves Scruff just as much as

Joey does. Someone who may be missing him terribly."

Mandy nodded and gulped but couldn't speak.

Jean got out the local telephone book. "I'll see if I can find the Browns' number and give them a call." She patted Mandy's hand again. "Perhaps you'd better warn Joey, just in case."

The door from the clinic swung open, and Mandy's mother came out. "If there are no urgent calls for me, I thought I'd —" She saw Mandy's face and stopped. "What's wrong, Mandy?" she asked.

Jean explained, and Dr. Emily gave Mandy a hug. "I know it's hard, but I think we ought to take care of this right away," she said.

Mandy sniffed. "Right *now*?"

"The sooner the better," said Dr. Emily. "I was going over to Walton to do some shopping, anyway. If you come with me, we'll stop at the house. Make sure it's the same dog."

Mandy sighed miserably. "Okay."

"And, darling, you'd better bring one of the signs," said Dr. Emily.

Mandy was quiet on the ride to Walton. In one way she wanted to get there quickly and find out the worst, but in another way she dreaded arriving there at all. The thought that she might be reuniting someone with a pet didn't make her feel much better, not when she thought about how much Joey loved Scruff. It would be *so* hard for them to be parted.

Dr. Emily decided to fill up with gas at the garage. "Then we'll leave the car here while we knock at the door of the Browns' house," she said. She glanced at Mandy. "It's best to know now, Mandy. The longer Joey has to get fond of Scruff, the harder it will be to say good-bye."

Mandy nodded silently. She knew this, of course, but it all seemed so unfair. Scruff loved Joey, and Joey loved him back. Joey needed Scruff, too. Needed him to watch out for him and protect him and be his ears . . .

As Dr. Emily drove into the garage, Mandy's

eyes were fixed on the house just beyond it, a square, modern building with a red front door and a rather messy yard. Had they or hadn't they lost a dog? *That* was the question.

Five minutes later, Mandy and her mother were making their way up the front path. Dr. Emily knocked, and two or three dogs began barking. A pleasant-looking young woman came to the door.

"Mrs. Brown?" Mandy's mother asked. Mandy crossed all her fingers and wished with all her might.

The woman shook her head. "No, I'm sorry," she said, "the Browns have moved down to Brighton."

"Oh!" Dr. Emily hesitated. "Did they move out very long ago?"

"About six weeks, I think. The house was empty for a couple of weeks, and then we moved in. Is there something I can help you with?"

Dr. Emily explained about Scruff, and

Mandy showed her the sign with the photo of him.

The woman looked at it carefully. "Well, I don't know whether this will be good news or bad news for you, but that *was* their dog."

Mandy's heart started beating fast.

"I know, because they left the poor little guy behind!" she continued. "Apparently they were going to an apartment in Brighton and couldn't keep a pet, so they just left him!"

"You're joking!" Dr. Emily said. "That's terrible."

"I agree entirely," said the woman. "We fed him for a couple of days, but we've got dogs of our own and couldn't take another one in. We were about to call the shelter when he disappeared. He just vanished into thin air. I had no idea where he went."

Mandy and her mother exchanged looks.

"We know where!" Mandy said, feeling so happy that she could have turned a cartwheel on the spot.

"Well, I hope it's a better home than he had with the Browns," said the woman. "Imagine just abandoning him here!"

"Oh, he *has* got a better home," said Mandy. "A *much* better home!"

9

Smart Dog!

"He's done it!"

"Good boy, Scruff!"

Mandy, James, and Joey jumped around the startled dog in delight. Joey opened a packet of doggy treats and put a whole pile on the floor.

"You smart dog!" he said, picking him up and hugging him.

Scruff, who'd already seen the chocolate treats, wriggled in Joey's arms. He couldn't see what all the fuss was about! All that had happened was that someone had rung the bell, so he'd alerted Joey and led him to the door. Easy!

"And all without really trying!" Mandy said.

She and James had turned up at Joey's house and rung the bell as usual, thinking that Mrs. Appleyard was in. She wasn't — but Scruff was!

"He must have remembered all his training from the other morning," James said.

Mandy nodded. "Suddenly it all made sense to him."

"He's the smartest dog in the world!" Joey said, hugging Scruff as he cleared the last few treats from the carpet.

Joey rolled onto the floor with Scruff, and the dog took some playful nips at Joey's sweatshirt, pulling it with his teeth. Joey pulled it back again, and Scruff growled and pretended to bite the material, acting as if the sweatshirt was alive and he was pouncing on it.

Mandy and James were just watching this and laughing when Mrs. Appleyard appeared.

"What's going on?" she said, looking alarmed. "Is that dog attacking Joey?"

Mandy quickly lifted Scruff off Joey. "They were just playing," she said.

Mrs. Appleyard frowned. "Is that what you call it? It sounded awful. Are you all right, Joey?"

Joey scrambled to his feet. "I'm fine, Mom. And you'll never guess what we've got to show you . . ."

Mrs. Appleyard frowned. "What's that on the carpet, Joey? Chocolate?"

Joey hastily rubbed at the mark with the cuff of his sweatshirt. "Just wait, Mom. You're going to be surprised. *Very* surprised."

"Am I really?" she said. "I suppose it's something to do with the dog."

"If you go outside again, we'll show you," said Mandy.

"But I just got here," Mrs. Appleyard objected. "I want to put the groceries away."

"Please come outside with me and Mandy for two minutes," James pleaded.

"It's really great, Mom!" said Joey.

At last Mrs. Appleyard agreed. She, Mandy, and James went outside, shutting the front door firmly behind them.

"We need to wait for a little while," Mandy said.

"Just to allow Scruff to settle down," added James.

Mrs. Appleyard looked confused. Mandy and James counted under their breath.

"Forty-nine . . . fifty!" Mandy said. She turned to Mrs. Appleyard. "Now will you please ring the doorbell?"

"Well, that won't do any good, will it?" said Mrs. Appleyard. "Why don't I just use my key to get in?"

James shook his head. "It's part of the surprise," he said.

Mrs. Appleyard shrugged but rang the bell anyway.

A moment later Joey, accompanied by Scruff, opened the door.

"Yes?" he said, beaming at his mother. "Did you ring?"

Mrs. Appleyard looked stunned. "How did you know I rang?" she asked.

"Scruff told me!" Joey said proudly. "He heard the bell, and he tapped me on the foot and led me to the door."

"Yes, but . . ."

"And before you say anything — I only opened it because I knew it was you!" Joey said. "I wouldn't open it to just anyone."

"Of course not," Mrs. Appleyard said, still looking stunned. She shook her head in amazement. "Well!" she said, "that's just marvelous." She stared down at Scruff and put out a hand as if she was going to pat him but pulled it away suddenly. "I suppose we have Mandy and James to thank for this?" she asked.

"And Joey and Scruff!" Mandy put in.

"Will he do it again?"

"Anytime you like!" said Mandy.

"Let's see," Mrs. Appleyard said. "Can I stay inside with Joey this time?"

"Of course you can," Mandy said.

Smiling broadly, Joey went back into the living room with Scruff. Mandy and Mrs. Appleyard went into the kitchen, and James went outside.

After a few moments he rang the bell. Mrs. Appleyard peeped around the kitchen door. When she saw Joey going off to answer it, a big smile lit up her face.

"I can hardly believe it," she said when everyone was together again. "You must have worked really hard to train him."

"So can I definitely keep him now?" Joey pleaded. "You wouldn't send him away now, would you?"

"Well, I . . ." Mrs. Appleyard began.

"And we know now that he doesn't belong to anyone else," Joey said persuasively. Mandy's mom had already called to tell Mrs. Appleyard what they'd discovered about Scruff's former owners.

Mrs. Appleyard looked down at Scruff. "He certainly *seems* all right, but I did say two weeks' trial, didn't I? He hasn't been living here a week yet."

"Oh, but Mom . . ." Joey began.

"That's enough, sweetie," Mrs. Appleyard said. "So far, so good, but it's still too early to say for sure."

10

Doggy Disgrace

James came over to Animal Ark after lunch. He had Blackie with him, and they were going to visit Joey and Scruff. They wanted the two dogs to get to know each other really well, so they were going to take them on a long walk up to Beacon Point and back.

Mandy had borrowed a collar and leash from

the clinic for Scruff, who didn't yet have his own. Mrs. Appleyard had promised to buy him a new collar and leash when his two weeks' trial was up.

As Mandy closed the door of her house behind her, Blackie jumped up on her, almost knocking her over.

"Down, boy!" James said. "Get down, you naughty thing!"

He put Blackie on his leash. "Maybe when Blackie sees how well Scruff is behaving, some of it will rub off on him!" he said.

Mandy ruffled Blackie's ears. "He's not that bad. He's still a puppy, really."

"I think he'll *always* be a puppy," James said, trying to hold Blackie back as they walked along.

When they got to Joey's house, Mrs. Appleyard told them that Joey was playing in the yard with Scruff. They went around to the back, and Blackie and Scruff ran up to each other, both of them bounding with excitement at the thought of playing together. They'd met twice before and had gotten along well. Blackie was much bigger than Scruff, of course, and between them they'd invented a game where Scruff ran under Blackie's legs and Blackie turned around and around in circles trying to catch him.

When they'd had about enough of that, Joey brought out two bowls of water. Blackie gulped his down, then pushed his nose into Scruff's bowl and finished that off, too.

Mandy, James, and Joey decided to take their walk. Scruff sat quietly while they put the borrowed collar on him. As Joey was putting on the leash, the front doorbell rang. Then came the noise of a dog yapping.

Before they could grab Scruff, he was running fast as a greyhound toward the yapping.

"What's happening?" said Joey, who hadn't heard a thing. "Why did he run off like that?"

"He heard a dog barking," Mandy explained, "at the front of the house." Just then came the horrible noise of two dogs yowling and snarling at each other, and someone shouting.

"Sounds like a fight!" James said fearfully. He touched Joey's arm. "Let's go!"

They hurried around to the front of the house, where they could see Joey's mom standing in the doorway. Outside on the step stood Mrs. Ponsonby, who'd just snatched up her Pekingese, Pandora. At her feet stood a fierce Scruff, looking up at Pandora and barking madly.

Mrs. Appleyard turned to see Joey and his friends. "Come and get this dog at once!" she cried. Mandy quickly turned to face Joey. "You'd better go and get Scruff!" she pointed.

Joey ran forward and picked up Scruff, who yapped once more and was quiet.

"Disgraceful!" Mrs. Ponsonby said, as her dog continued to bark. "That dog attacked us for no good reason."

"He appeared out of nowhere," Mrs. Appleyard said, flustered. "Really, I can't apologize enough, Mrs. Ponsonby."

"People ought to keep their dogs under con-

trol," Mrs. Ponsonby said. "Upsetting my Pandora like this . . ."

"I really am very sorry," Mrs. Appleyard said. "I don't know what's the matter with him. He didn't actually hurt your dog though, did he? Just made a lot of noise."

"He frightened Pandora to death!" Mrs. Ponsonby said.

"Oh, but he was just defending his territory," Mandy said, feeling that she couldn't keep quiet a moment longer. "He thought Pandora was a threat. He was defending us."

Mrs. Appleyard frowned. "Well, the other dog in the garden — your Blackie — didn't feel the need to leap at Pandora, did he? He's still sitting there quietly."

"That's because it's not *his* territory that was being threatened," Mandy explained.

"And anyway, Scruff was just barking," Joey argued. "He wouldn't have hurt anyone!"

"We're not sure of that," Mrs. Appleyard said. She took a deep breath. "I really can't risk having our visitors threatened in this way."

She turned her attention to Mrs. Ponsonby and smiled rather shakily. "But won't you come in?" she said. "We can have a nice peaceful cup of tea in the living room."

"How kind," said Mrs. Ponsonby and, holding Pandora like a precious piece of china, she entered the house.

Mandy, James, and Joey followed Mrs. Appleyard into the kitchen.

"Honestly, Scruff wouldn't hurt a fly," Mandy said anxiously.

"And we're going to teach him to alert Joey to alarm bells next!" said James.

Joey looked at his mother, waiting to see what she was going to say.

Mrs. Appleyard filled the kettle with water and then turned to face Joey. "I'm sorry, darling," she said, "I don't think we can keep him."

Joey gave a little cry.

"I can't have a dog like that around. I don't know what he's going to do next. I just wouldn't feel safe."

Tears filled Joey's eyes. "But —" he began.

"I'm sorry, Joey," his mother said, "but I've made up my mind. He can stay for the weekend, but after that you'll have to find him a new home."

"Oh, Mom —" Joey started to say.

"And that's absolutely final," his mother said.

11

Scruff to the Rescue

"It's just so sad," Mandy said to her grandma later that day in Lilac Cottage. "I mean, Scruff wouldn't have hurt Pandora, he really wouldn't. He was just being noisy."

"I know, dear," Grandma said. "Some dogs — well, it's true what they say, isn't it? — their bark is worse than their bite."

Mandy nodded slowly.

"It is *very* sad, though," Grandma said. "Especially since you were getting along so well with Scruff's training." She poured Mandy a glass of orange juice. "What will happen to him now?"

Mandy sighed. "Mom and Dad said that the animal shelter will take him."

Grandma nodded. "They'll find a good home for him."

"But he's already *got* a good home," said Mandy. She sighed again. "Oh, I wish Mrs. Ponsonby hadn't come over when we were in the yard. She always makes a mess of things. Or that she'd come over without Pandora. Or that . . ."

"Now don't upset yourself," Grandma said. "Why don't you go into the garden and get Grandpa to pick the last of the pole beans to take home with you."

Mandy looked doubtful. "Thank you very much, but Dad said he's eaten all the beans he can possibly manage. He said he thinks he's changing into a pole bean."

Grandma chuckled. "To tell you the truth, I'm a little tired of them myself. I've already got twenty bags in the freezer. At this rate, we won't need to plant any next year!"

"Anyway, I'm on my way to James's house now," Mandy said. "And then we're going to visit Joey and try to cheer him up. James says he's going to let him share Blackie."

"That's nice of James," Grandma said. "Though I can't see *that* scamp of a pup learning to be a hearing dog!"

"Neither can I," Mandy said. "That's why Scruff was so great."

Grandma gave her a hug. "Now, remember! No gloomy faces in front of Joey. He's going to need cheering up more than you."

Mandy managed a smile. "I know, Grandma. I'll try to be cheerful when we get there, really I will . . ."

Mandy and James were quiet and deep in thought as they walked along Main Street toward Joey's house. It was only when they got near the general store that James spoke.

"Maybe we should get Joey some candy or something," he said.

"Good idea," Mandy nodded. "It might make him feel a little better."

"It might," James said, "but I don't think so. I know how I'd feel if my mom said I had to get rid of Blackie."

Mandy shook her head. "Poor Joey," she said.

"And poor Scruff," added James.

They were coming out of the general store after buying candy when Mandy suddenly caught hold of James's arm.

"There's Joey now!" she said, pointing up the road, "walking toward the green."

They walked faster to catch up with Joey, knowing that it was useless to call him.

"It looks as if he's already been trying to cheer himself up," James said. "He's bought himself an ice cream."

"And Scruff is trotting along behind him!" Mandy said.

As Mandy spoke, a car came from the direction of the green and began to make its way toward Main Street. It was going very fast.

Joey, intent on his ice cream and feeling so miserable that he wasn't thinking about what he was doing, stepped off the sidewalk.

The driver honked, but Joey didn't hear it and took another step forward. Mandy clutched James's arm in fright.

"Joey!" Mandy cried. She and James started running down the street.

The car honked again, long and loud. Then there was a loud screech of brakes as it tried to stop. Scruff, who had heard Mandy call Joey's name, took a flying leap at Joey's ankle and held onto his jeans with his teeth.

Joey fell over onto his ice cream, and the car jolted to a halt, turning sideways across the street. By the time Mandy and James arrived, panting, Mrs. Appleyard, who was just coming out of the general store, and three other people had arrived at the scene.

Joey was helped to his feet, and Mrs. Apple-

yard clutched him tightly. "What were you *doing*? You crossed the street without looking, didn't you?" she said. Then she burst into tears, hugging Joey very tightly. Joey wriggled uncomfortably, feeling that he could hardly breathe.

The driver of the car got out. "Silly kid," he muttered.

"You were going too fast!" one of the bystanders said accusingly.

"That boy wasn't looking where he was going!" the driver retorted.

Joey, who was looking bewildered, nodded. "No, I wasn't," he said. "I was eating my ice cream and thinking about poor Scruff . . ."

Mandy took a tissue out of her pocket and wiped some ice cream from Joey's jeans. "Are you all right?" she asked. "We saw it — James and I saw everything. Scruff heard me shout your name — and he saved you!"

Joey, suddenly realizing exactly what had happened, struggled out of his mother's arms.

"Scruff!" he said, looking around frantically for his dog. "Scruff saved me!"

Scruff, intent on licking ice cream from anywhere he could, didn't even look up.

Mrs. Appleyard, white-faced, nodded. "Yes, that's right. I saw it, too. He did save your life!"

"That dog's a hero!" one of the onlookers remarked.

When the little drama was over, the people who'd gathered at the scene went on their way. The driver made sure Joey was all right, muttered a few more words about it not being *his* fault, and got back into his car and drove off.

Mandy, James, Joey, and his mom just stood there, looking down at Scruff.

"Scruff's a hero," Joey said.

"Yes, he is," Mandy agreed.

Joey looked up at his mom. "So do you think I can keep him, Mom?"

Mrs. Appleyard couldn't stop hugging Joey. "Yes, you can, darling," she said. "How could we ever get rid of him now?" She straightened up and took a deep breath. "Now, why don't

we all go to the pet shop in Walton and buy Scruff a collar and leash of his own? And a basket and anything else you think he might need. Mandy, you know about things like that, don't you?"

Mandy nodded, her eyes shining.

Joey picked up Scruff and buried his face in his fur. "I can keep you!" he said. "You're mine forever!"